For my family

Published By Priya Desai

Priya Desai
Box 226
30 Red Lion Street
Richmond upon Thames
Surrey
TW9 1RB
www.priyadesai.co.uk

ISBN 978-0-9565247-0-6

Designed by Flit, London
www.flitlondon.co.uk

Illustrations by Emma Hockley
www.emmahockleyarts.co.uk

British Library Cataloguing in Publication Data
A catalogue record of this book is available from the British Library

Printed in the UK by Empress Litho, London
www.empresslitho.com

Benjamin Writer-Messy

Once upon a time, there was a place called Pencil Land. Pencil Land was a very special place. Everything that you saw, in one way or another looked like a pencil! Every car, every house, every shop, even every person!

And every building was bright and beautiful. Some people even say that all the colours of the world could be found in Pencil Land.

2B

This is a story about Benjamin Writer–Messy. Now, just in case you are wondering about Benjamin's funny name. You should know that everyone in Pencil Land liked to write and was also GOOD at writing. That's why everyone in Pencil Land had Writer as their middle name. The most famous people in Pencil Land were Mr Robert Writer–Magnificently Perfect and Mrs Writer–Absolutely Beautiful. Now, back to Benjamin Writer–Messy. Benjamin or Ben as he liked to be called was a very happy little boy. He had lots of friends and he was so talented. He could ride a bike. He could play football and swim. He was good at cutting. He could make a sandwich and he could just about sing but he could not WRITE!

This made Ben feel sad. Every night before he went to bed he would pray, "Please, please make my handwriting better tomorrow."

In Pencil Land children
went to school on topsy turvy
days or you could very simply say, every
other day if you wanted to be precise. So that
meant Benjamin Writer-Messy went to school on

**Monday, Wednesday, Friday,
and every Sunday!**

You may be wondering why this was. Well, Pencil Land was a very special and also unusual place, not like the place you and I live in. Pencil Land was ruled by the Handwriting Queen and a long, long time ago she decided that she wanted her kingdom to be different and all children should go to school on topsy turvy days but there was one very important rule that children needed to follow – everyone had to do **two** hours of homework on their home days!

One Wednesday morning, Benjamin Writer–Messy arrived at school. Everyone seemed busy and he was not sure why. He saw his best friend, Sam Writer-Good whizz past him. "Sam," shouted Ben, "Why are you rushing?"

"I am getting ready for the handwriting competition on Friday Ben," said Sam.

"The handwriting competition?" said Ben.

"Yes, the handwriting competition, don't you remember Mrs Writer-Beautiful telling us about it on Monday? said Sam.

"No....I must have been dreaming," said Ben.

"Well, I have to dash, I need to find a good sharpener to sharpen all my pencils so I can practise my handwriting at break time," said Sam.

"OH NO," thought Benjamin Writer–Messy. "What am I going to do? A handwriting competition on Friday. I find handwriting so hard, no matter how hard I try. No one can ever read my handwriting. I will never win the handwriting competition..."

Benjamin Writer–Messy heard the bell ring. It was time for his first lesson of the day – HANDWRITING. He walked slowly along the hallway to his classroom. His mind was racing and all he could think about was rushing home to practise his handwriting. He knew that he would have to practise really hard if anyone was going to be able to read his handwriting on Friday at the competition.

Mrs Writer–Teacher was in an excited mood, "Well children, today we are going over the rules for the handwriting competition which is on Friday. Firstly all of you must enter the competition! Did you hear that Benjamin Writer–Messy?"

"Yes Mrs Writer–Teacher," said Ben.

Handwriting Competition

1. Your name
2. The date
3. Write something about yourself. For example, something about your favourite book, or your favourite toy.

"For the competition you all have to write your name, the date and something about yourself. For example, what your favourite book is or what your favourite toy is and why. After the competition, Mr Writer–Headmaster will decide who has the best handwriting and whoever wins the competition will receive the school handwriting trophy. Benjamin, I suggest you spend all of Thursday practising your handwriting for Friday's competition."

After school that day Ben went home a little worried, in fact very worried but he tried to look as if he was only a little worried so his mum would not get worried as well.

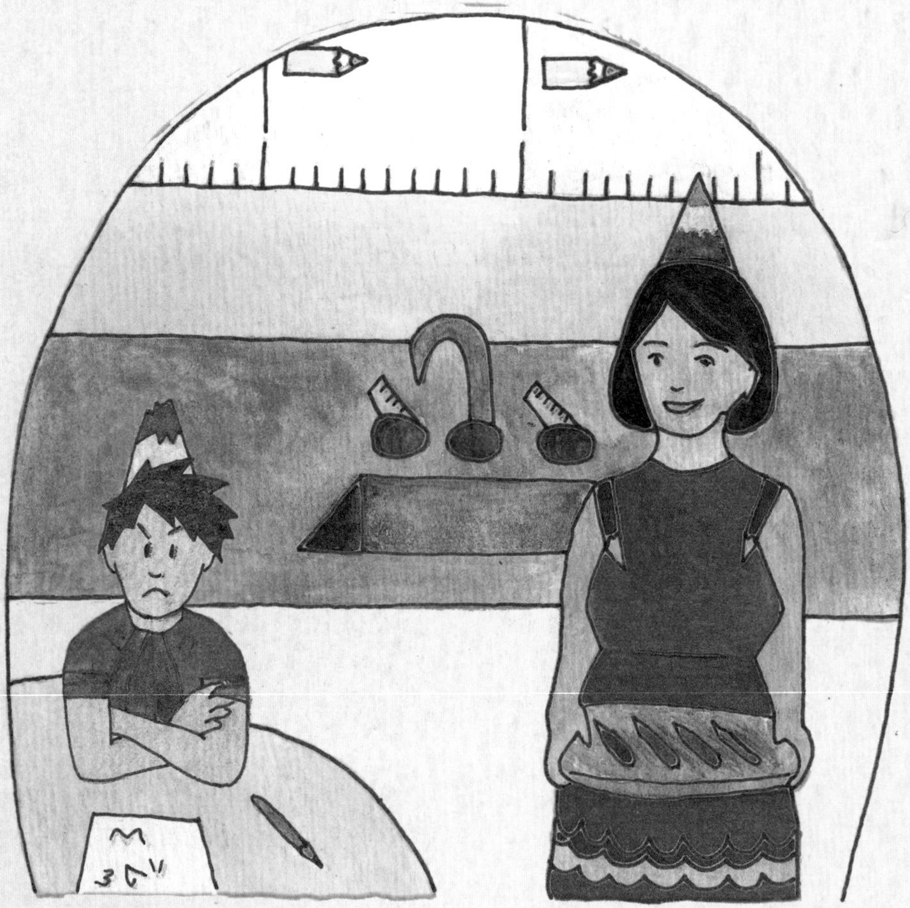

He sat down to have his afterschool snack. “Here you go Ben. I have made you special cookies shaped like your school pencils,” said Ben’s mum excitedly.

“Mum, why does everything have to be pencil shaped?” shouted Ben.
“Of course everything must be pencil shaped Ben! We live in Pencil Land,” said Ben’s mum.

“Yes Ben we live in Pencil Land,” said his older brother Alex Writer–Great, “I think you should start practising your handwriting straightaway because no one can ever read it! I’m already good at handwriting and don’t need to practise but your need ALL the help you can get! I think I’ll go and play football at Pencil Stadium, seeya later.”

That evening, Ben had a go at writing the alphabet to practise his letter shapes but he just found it too hard!

Ben went to bed that night and all he could do was toss and turn. He knew he had to think of a plan and find a way of becoming good at handwriting before the competition. He got up out of bed and walked to the window. It was a dark night but in the distance he could see a cluster of bright lights. It was the most magical, heavenly place in the whole of Pencil Land, the Handwriting Queen's palace. Then Ben knew what he had to do.

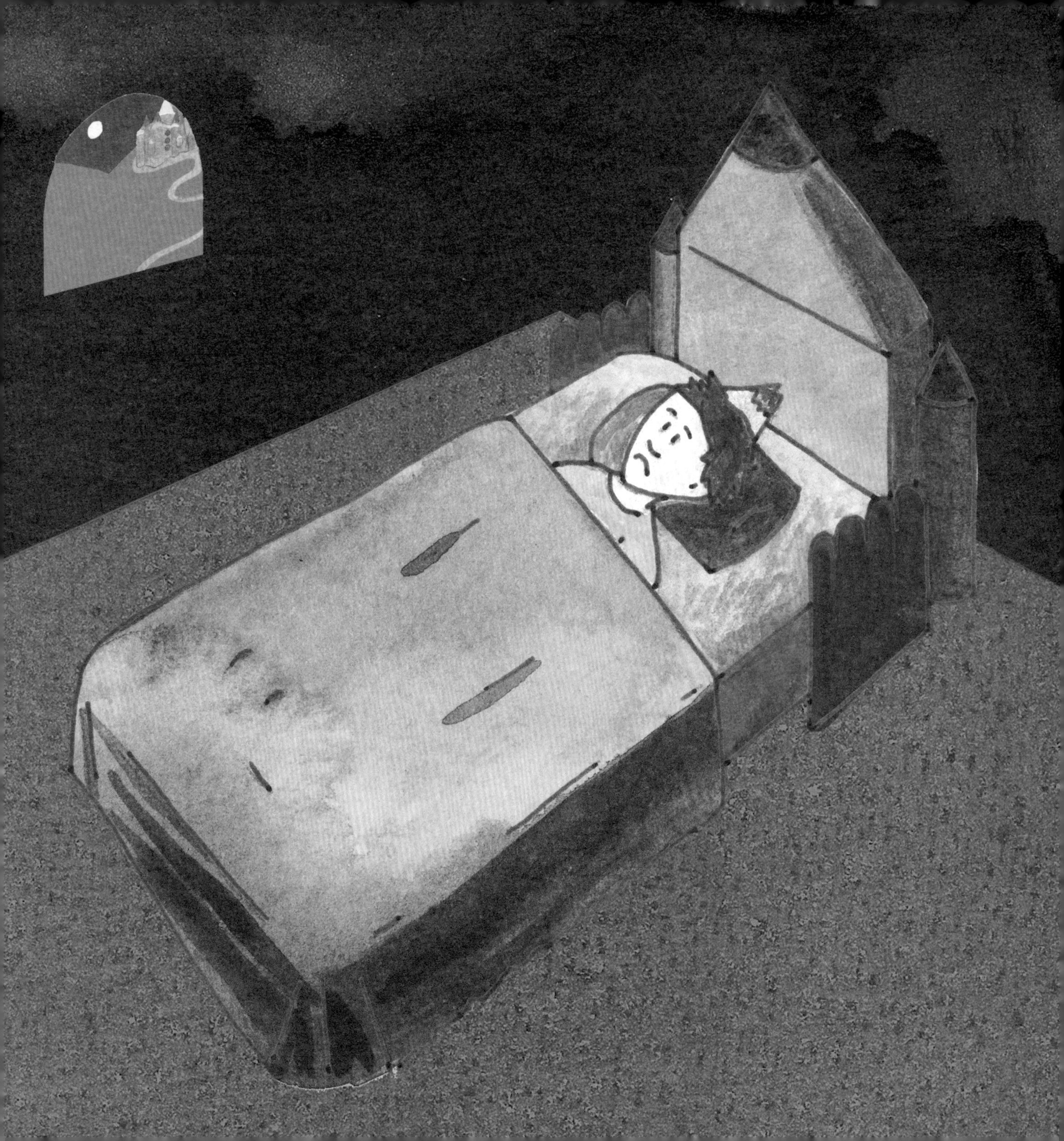

The next morning Ben rushed out of the house. “Bye mum,” he said

“Where are you going Ben?” shouted his mum.

But he did not hear her.

Ben rode his bike along the narrow path of Pencil Tree Forest. He had never been so far away from his home before and he felt a little scared. He pedalled as fast as he could and before he knew it he was racing down a steep hill and the trees of Pencil Tree Forest were far behind him. All of a sudden he lost control! Ben couldn't slow down. He closed his eyes. Ben had crashed.

He slowly opened his eyes and before him he saw a magnificent, sparkly fence. He had made it.

The Hand Writing Queen's Palace was more beautiful than he could have ever imagined. Every pencil that made up the walls sparkled with jewels and diamonds and all of a sudden Ben felt very small and unimportant but he knew that he could not turn back now.

Ben walked up to the large pencil shaped door of the palace. "Here goes," said Ben to himself as he rang the enormous bell. No one answered. Ben tried again. No one answered. Ben tried again. This time he heard footsteps and then an old, angry voice asking, "Yes, who is there?"

“My name is Benjamin
Writer–Messy,” shouted Ben.
“I have come to visit the Handwriting Queen,”
said Benjamin.

“The Queen does not accept visitors. Good Bye young man,”
said the old, angry voice.

“But I have got to see the Queen!” shouted Ben as he heard the footsteps of the scary voice fade away.

Ben knew that he had to somehow get into the palace. He looked around him...maybe a window...maybe he could climb through a window...no, none were open...maybe he could climb up a pencil wall...no...the diamonds and jewels were so sparkly that they would blind him and he would fall. “Mmm,” he thought. At that very moment a grey, large, fat cat creept out of the pencil door cat flap. “That’s it,” thought Ben. “I’ll crawl though the cat flap.”

Ben got down on his knees. He gently pushed his head and arms through the cat flap and then squeezed the rest of his body through. He was in!! He looked up, the Hand Writing Queens Palace was dazzling and all along the walls were beautifully shaped letters and words.

Ben suddenly heard a beautiful voice singing.
It was coming from upstairs.

Ben quietly began to creep
up the stairs. He felt weightless
as he tiptoed up, lost in the beauty of the
Queen's mesmerising voice. Suddenly there she was
standing in front of him. The Handwriting Queen!
Ben was speechless.

"Hello, young man, come closer," said the Hand–Writing Queen, as
she stood waiting at the top of the stairs.

"How did you get here?" asked the Queen.

"The angry...I mean the nice man downstairs would not let me in so I snuck
in through the cat flap," said Ben nervously.

"Oh, how very clever of you. What is your name?" asked the Queen kindly.
As quiet as a mouse Ben said, "It's...it's Benjamin Writer–Messy."

"What an interesting name....why are you here?" asked the Queen.
Ben found the courage to look up at the Queen and said, "Your Majesty. I
really need your help to become good at handwriting.
Will you help me please?"

The Queen looked at
Ben warmly and asked,

"Ben why do you find writing so hard?"

"Well your majesty, I always try and practise but when my pencil touches the paper the letter shapes are never right and then no one can read my handwriting. I have to make my handwriting better, there is a competition at school tomorrow," said Ben.

"Oh dear," said the Queen. "Ben, you will become a great handwriter one day. Handwriting is all about being careful and slow. The letters form beautiful shapes. The beautifully shaped letters form words and the words look like drawings. The words form sentences and the sentences make one big beautiful picture. Ben I have something which can help you. Close your eyes Ben."

Ben heard the sound of footsteps, and then what sounded like a drawer openning and closing. "Okay Ben you can open your eyes," said the Queen.

The Queen held out a golden pencil. "Take this golden pencil Ben. I want you to use this pencil in the competition tomorrow. I wish you the best of luck and remember Ben, dreams can come true," said the Queen.

Ben left the Handwriting Queen's palace and immediately placed his golden pencil inside his jacket pocket. He could not believe that he had just met the most famous person in the whole of Pencil Land.

The next day Ben arrived at school and went straight to his classroom. “Hi Ben are you ready for the competition?”asked Sam Writer–Good.

“Yes Sam. I am,” said Ben confidently.

Ben sat at his desk and placed his golden pencil in front of him. All his friends could not stop admiring his dazzling golden pencil.

He heard the 9 O’clock bell. HE WAS READY!

“Right children”, said Mrs Writer–Teacher “You have 30 minutes to complete your handwriting for the competition. Remember write your name, the date and something about yourself. We will start after our count down from ten.

"Ten, nine, eight, seven, six, five, four, three, two, one

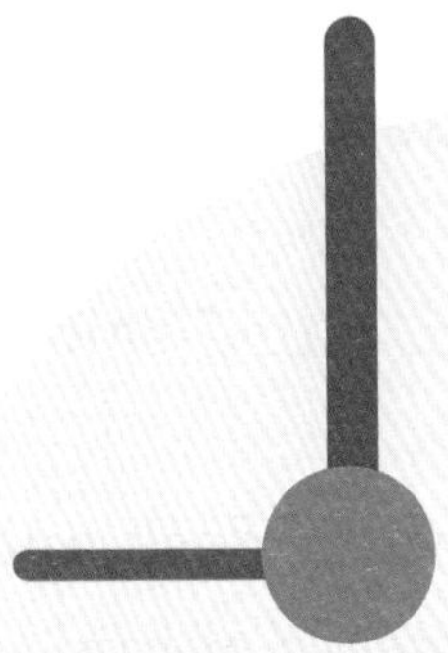

...You may begin."
Ben picked up his golden pencil and carefully and slowly, wrote his name,

'BENJAMIN WRITER–MESSY'

and then he carefully and slowly wrote the date. He looked at his work. The Handwriting Queen was right. His handwriting was beautiful and all his letter shapes were perfect. He continued to write.

"I never used to like
handwriting. I always used to practise
but practising never helped me. Maybe I tried
too hard and wrote too fast. Maybe I worried about
my handwriting too much and didn't believe in myself.
A special friend told me to be careful and slow. Now I write
carefully and slowly. My handwriting feels like magic. I'm looking
at my handwriting right now and my letter shapes are beautiful. I
feel proud of my work. I love handwriting now."

At 9.30 am Mrs Writer–Teacher rang a bell. The competition was over. "The winner of the competition will be announced at 12 O'clock," said Mrs Writer–Teacher.

Ben felt fantastic! He ran outside and played in the playground with all his friends. For the first time ever he was not worried about his handwriting and what it looked like.

Out came Mr Writer–Headmaster. "Children you have all worked very hard today! You all have beautiful handwriting. However one person's handwriting has stood out the most." Ben closed his eyes. He felt so nervous that he covered his eyes with his hands.

"BENJAMIN WRITER–MESSY," said Mr Writer–Headmaster.

Ben's eyes were still closed. He thought he had heard his name but he was not sure because he had also heard lots of children gasp and some even scream!

"BENJAMIN WRITER–MESSY! You have won!" said Mr Writer–Headmaster.

Ben opened one eye. "Me?"

"Yes Ben," said Mr Writer–Head Headmaster.

Ben was speechless. He opened his other eye. "Me?"

"Ben you can write beautifully now. You must have practised very hard. This makes me feel proud of you! This trophy is yours. It is a very special trophy because it has come from the Handwriting Queen's Palace," said Mr Writer–Headmaster.

Ben gratefully took the trophy and hugged it. Ben felt amazing.

That evening Ben went to bed and he knew that tomorrow was going to be an amazing day because now he could write just like all his friends. Ben thought that maybe he should change his name to *Benjamin Writer–Messy–Nomore.*

Yes he liked the sound of that name.

Acknowledgements

Mum and Dad for always encouraging me, understanding me, supporting me and for all the hugs and sending me the right way.

Hital for being you. Your request came true.

Emma, the wonderful illustrator for being there from day one, sharing my excitement, spreading the excitement and seeing Benjamin.

Paul for his endless enthusiasm, encouragement, dedication and vision.

With special thanks to all the lovely people and children that I work with.

And to my friends, you know who you are.